GOLD CLIFF HOUSE

WINDY HILL

SILVER CLIFF

SANDCASTLE BAY

N
W   E
S

GOLD CLIFF

SILVER CREEK

PINENEEDLE WOOD

SANDSTONE ROAD

To SANDPIPER ISLAND

THE TREE HOUSE

THE SANDPIT

FISHING BOAT ROW

SILVER CREEK MOUTH

SANDY EDGE CLIFF

THE RABBITS' HOUSE

SILVER CORNER

THE HEDGEHOGS' HOUSE

THE ELEPHANTS' HOUSE

SANDBANK LANE

SANDPIT STEPS

THE ZEBRAS' HOUSE

SILVER STREET

SEAGULL ROCKS

LAPPING WATER BEACH

THE VILLAGE OF
SANDY EDGE

LAPPING WATER LAKE

For Rachel and Helen

With special thanks to
Lucy, Helen, David, Amelia and Liz

First published 1995 by Walker Books Ltd
87 Vauxhall Walk, London SE11 5HJ

2 4 6 8 10 9 7 5 3 1

© 1995 Penny Dale

This book has been typeset in Horley Old Style.

Printed in Italy

British Library Cataloguing in Publication Data
A catalogue record for this book is
available from the British Library.

ISBN 0-7445-3782-7

Daisy Rabbit's
TREE HOUSE

Penny Dale

WALKER BOOKS
AND SUBSIDIARIES
LONDON • BOSTON • SYDNEY

This is the village of Sandy Edge, which lies beside Lapping Water Lake. All sorts of animals live here, so there are all sorts of houses. On summer days you'll find many animals playing down by the water.

In a lane that winds up from the shore
is the Rabbits' green grassy house. Here are
Mr and Mrs Rabbit, Daisy Rabbit and her
little brother Digger. They live next door to
the Hedgehogs' prickly brown house.

There is a tree house in the Rabbits' back garden.

Here is Daisy Rabbit getting ready to camp out in

it for the night, with her friends Nelly

Jumbo, Deborah Zebra and

Nipper Hedgehog. It is

their favourite thing to do.

Not long ago Daisy felt homesick sleeping any-

where but in her own bed. Once she stayed at Nelly

Jumbo's house. At first everything was fine. She

had a lovely big tea and a splashy bath in the sink.

But at bedtime she felt a bit sad.

She lay in her jumbo hammock and thought

of her own little bed at home, with all her

pictures round it. She didn't say anything,

but she wished she was there instead.

Another time Daisy stayed at Deborah
Zebra's house. At first she had a wonderful
time. They dressed up as fairies and later
they played hide-and-seek
under the table.

But at bedtime Daisy felt sad again.

She looked around at Deborah and all the

little Zebras, and it made her think how much

she missed Digger. She didn't say anything,

but she wished she was with him instead.

Then Daisy stayed at Nipper Hedgehog's house.

At first she was very happy. But at bedtime

she suddenly missed her

mother so much, she couldn't help crying.

The Hedgehogs were very kind to her.

Mr Hedgehog gave her a great big prickly

hedgehog hug and Nipper brought her a drink.

Then Mrs Hedgehog tucked her up gently.

"Sleep well, Daisy," whispered Nipper.

The next day Daisy felt better and when she got home she told her mum everything.

"I don't think I can stay the night with my friends any more," she said.

Mrs Rabbit thought, then she had an idea.

"What if you all slept in the tree house?" she asked.

"Maybe you wouldn't feel homesick there."

So that's what they did. And Daisy didn't

feel homesick a bit. Everyone had tea. Everyone

had baths. Then Daisy, Nelly, Deborah, Nipper

and Digger all snuggled up in the tree house.

Mrs Rabbit read them a story.

"Once upon a time," she began…

And at the end of the story, Mrs Rabbit
turned down the lantern and tiptoed gently
away down the garden.

When she looked back, what did she see?

Five little friends in the soft summer moonlight,

all fast asleep in the tree house.

"Good night," she whispered.